Dear friends,
I hope this book
finds a "special" place
in your heart.
Happy Reading,
Susan Vernick

Danny's Special Collection

Susan A. Vernick

Susan A. Vernick

Illustrated by Natalie G. Smith

White Bird Publications
P.O Box 90145
Austin, Texas 78709
www.whitebirdpublications.com

Copyright©2019 by Susan A. Vernick
Illustrations by Natalie G. Smith

ISBN: 978-1-63363-392-6
LCCN: 2019940120

PRINTED IN THE UNITED STATES OF AMERICA

To Jesus, my Lord and Savior.

To my husband, John and my four children: John, Anna, Lauren, and Benjamin for their dedication, encouragement, love and support.

To my father and mother, Ed and Natalie Smith, and my triplet sisters: Sandy Smith and Sharon Petrakis who also dearly loved Danny. Thank you all for reading and editing this story and encouraging me on this journey. A special thanks to my mom, Natalie, who illustrated this book.

To those who also loved and cared for Danny: Grandpa and Grandma Smith, Nana and Papa Girardi, Aunt Mil, Aunt Barb, Aunt Betty, and cousins too many to list on the "Smith" and "Girardi" side of my family.

To my Uncle Frank Girardi who always made Danny "Dan the Man" feel like one of the boys.

To my Aunt "Cici" Girardi, who adored Danny and always encouraged me to write.

There were many days my brother and I would go for long walks behind our house. There were tall oak trees, maple trees, and pine trees as far as we could see. There was also a beautiful pasture and an old, white barn in the field behind us. We would pick apples without anyone knowing. Sometimes we found pears, nuts, and berries. It was peaceful and still, and we loved our walks.

Even though my brother was older, I would often go with him. He had a way of seeing the world in a different way. Everyone seemed to race around, in a hurry. Not, Danny; he was consistent, steady, and able to appreciate so much of what I missed, especially during our walks. He was not always included with friends his age. So, our time together was special to him and to me.

One day Danny began collecting on our walks. This was a new adventure. We went early one Saturday morning, and he began collecting stones: large, rough stones, grey, black, and orange-speckled stones. He even picked-up lucky stones and pebbles. They shimmered in the sunlight in a small stream, and Danny just kept picking them up. I asked him why he was collecting them, and he said, "For a special reason, for a special person."

Another day, we walked in the late afternoon. It was overcast and cool that day. We could smell the evergreens so strongly. Danny began collecting pinecones, an armful of them. Some still had sap on them, and small branches were even attached. He did not care that they were sticky and messy. He wore a Pittsburgh football jersey with his favorite team colors, and the pinecones just stuck to it. Danny laughed, and so did I. He smelled them and carried as many as he could in his arms. I asked to help. "No," Danny said. He wanted to do it himself. I asked, "Why? He said, "They were for a special reason, for a special person."

Then, one breezy, warm afternoon we went for another walk. Danny once again began collecting. It was twigs and sticks on this particular day. Now that was fun! The twigs "snapped" as we walked through the woods collecting them. There were large, rough ones and small, green ones-all sizes, shapes, and textures. He brought a large brown bag on this particular day. I asked if I could help. He shook his head and said, "It is for a special reason, for a special person."

Natalie G. Smith

It was evening, and Danny wanted to walk again. Today, he had a cardboard box with him and wanted to stop at a friend's house. Danny invited his friend to walk with us. The boy had practice soon, so we sat on his porch instead and talked for a while. We then started our walk. We walked further than usual that day, but Danny didn't seem to collect anything. He just opened the box and walked around a small field as the wind rustled the overgrown grass. Then, he closed it tightly and said, "For a special reason, for a special person." And we were done for the day and walked home.

A gorgeous, sunny day greeted us. Danny woke me early and asked me to go for a walk with him. He brought his baseball glove and ball that day, for no apparent reason. But, he had to have them. I suggested that he leave them behind, and he got frustrated and was quiet during our walk. I even found myself feeling irritated with him, as I sometimes did, but once I saw the beautiful flowers he picked, that all went away. He picked Black-eyed Susans, wild-daisies, and Queens-Anne's lace. He even found wild violets that day. When he was finished, the bouquet looked like one from a florist. Not even a trained eye could have done better. Yes, the stems were different lengths, some drooped, but the colors were amazing. That day Danny raced home, his collection was now complete. I could hear him saying over and over again, as he walked in front of me, "It's for a special reason, for a special person."

Danny walked into the house and went straight up to his room. My grandparents were visiting that day, as they often did. He came down with all of his collections, each collection he had placed in separate boxes.

Danny handed the rock collection to my father, paused and said, "These are for you, dad." As my dad lifted the rocks out of the box, one by one, out fell a small, torn, green paper, on it was written..." You are my rock. You help me to be strong." We all paused for a moment, and then I knew what Danny meant. I knew what was in Danny's heart. He simply meant, "Dad, you are my rock, and you help me to be strong and solid when things are tough. You also teach me to not let anyone walk on me, like these stones are walked on, and for that, I am unbreakable and strong." I shared that with my family, and they all listened as Danny handed out the next collection.

Danny handed the twigs to grandma and grandpa. Danny stumbled over his words a bit and said, "These are yours because I am like a branch from your tree." As they sorted through the branches, out fell a note on a scrap of brown bag paper that said what Danny had just told our grandparents. Looking down at the box, our grandparents realized the meaning of Danny's collection. We knew again exactly what Danny meant. "Because of both of you, I am strong. I am like a branch that comes from a large, strong family tree. When I feel broken like these branches, you make me feel whole again like a big, beautiful oak tree. Even when I feel torn down or broken like these branches, I can look at these and remember the family tree that I come from."

"Sis, these are for you," Danny said. I stared at the collection and knew what Danny meant to say as he handed me the pinecones. I, too, finally fully understood his reason for collecting. Looking like it was ripped from an old envelope, the note inside read..." You stick by me, always, always." My heart was filled with emotions as I knew what the pinecones meant to Danny. "You always stick by my side, and you are my protector. Like these pinecones with their sap, you stick by me. And, like these evergreens provide protection in the winter, you protect me. Even when it is difficult to be my sister, you are always there by my side."

Then, Danny pulled out the cardboard box and set it on the table. Taped to the top of the box was a piece of torn notebook paper. On it was written, "My friend, you are like the wind." We paused for a moment and realized what he was saying about our neighbor. "I cannot see the wind, but I feel it, and it wraps around me. Although, we are not always together, I feel our friendship, and it surrounds me, and I know it is always there, like the wind." Then Danny opened the box quickly, smiled, and said, "The wind...feel it?"

"Mom, here these are yours," Danny said. "You will like these-they are pretty and different."

As she smelled the flowers, Mom also understood his special collections. On a small piece of a sticky-pad paper, these words were written, "You think I am beautiful, and perfect like these flowers." Again, we could hear Danny's heart. "Mom, you always see me as beautiful and colorful like these flowers. Even when I feel down, like a droopy flower, or stick out in a crowd like these flowers of different lengths; you always think I am beautiful, even though I am different."

With amazement, we read our notes again, and then we thanked Danny for our beautiful collections. They were most precious to each of us. We could see that Danny was inspired. He grabbed his favorite brown jacket, without saying a word. With great determination and a slight smile on his face; Danny had another plan. "Come on sis; let's walk." As we opened the door and stepped onto the back porch, the crisp air hit our faces, the smell of the outdoors surrounded us, and we began our walk again.

CPSIA information can be obtained
at www.ICGtesting.com
Printed in the USA
BVHW021410060719
552763BV00019B/135/P